QUEEN
SARDINE

in Kitten
chaos

By the same author

Queen Sardine
Queen Sardine and Princess Persia

QUEEN
SARDINE
in Kitten Chaos

Kate Willis-Crowley

templar

A TEMPLAR BOOK

First published in the UK by Templar Publishing,

part of the Bonnier Publishing Group,

Northburgh House, 10 Northburgh Street, London EC1V 0AT

www.bonnier.com

Text and illustrations © Kate Willis Crowley 2015

The moral rights of the author have been asserted.

A CIP catalogue record for this book is available from the British Library.

ISBN: 978-1-78370-207-7

1 3 5 7 9 10 8 6 4 2

Printed and bound by Clays Ltd, St Ives Plc

For Isis, my ~~mews~~ muse

SCARED

Shuffle, snap, thunk...

What was that? Who's there? I pull my blanket up over my nose and peek out. My bedroom's a shadowy fuzz as I blink the sleep from my eyes. Nothing moves. Still, I know I didn't imagine it – there is something alive in here, creeping around in my bedroom... But I'm not scared! I'm not scared, I'm not scared...

"Mum? Is that you?"

My wardrobe door creaks as something scuttles past it, shuffling towards me. It's definitely not Mum. The shadow looks cat-sized and cat-shaped. . . It must be Queen Sardine then! That'll be it – it's probably just my furry, feline, best-ever friend dropping in for a late-night cuddle.

There's no need to panic. I'm fine. Totally 100% calm and okay, and – erm, I'm definitely not scared.

Scratch... Scratch...

"Your M-Majesty?" I mumble, still half asleep.

"Yes, I'm right here, silly Ivy," answers Queen Sardine from the end of my bed. "Now please stop fussing, I'm trying to sleep." But something isn't right about this.

"Was that you who just came in?" I ask.

I mean, don't get me wrong, I'm pleased it's Queen Sardine. She is my favourite neighbour and comes to visit all the time.

Mum put a cat flap in the kitchen door so she can let herself in whenever she wants. And she comes by so often, it was bound to be her. But something's not adding up here. She's already made herself comfy on my bed – that was quick! And she's nestled into the bend of my knees like she's been there all night. Weird.

"Mmm. . ." she replies, which means she's not really listening.

"Y-your Majesty. . ." I say, and my throat's so dry and tight that the sound kind of croaks out of me. "What were you doing over by my wardrobe just now?"

I wriggle till I can see her in the blurry

darkness. Her eyes are shut, but she stretches, yawns, and answers me anyway: "Ivy, you're imagining things. I've been right here with you for hours."

Queen Sardine's been right here for hours? Then who or what is in my room?

Fine – I admit it now – I am scared, okay? I'm scared of the dark. Scared of the night. And most of all I'm scared of the stinking, drooling monsters that slither into my imagination when I'm sleepy.

Scratch... Sniff...

But that noise wasn't my imagination, there is something here! Something rotten and bony and bug-eyed and stink-tongued and definitely, absolutely, TOTALLY, probably about to eat us. . . And it sounds like it's over in the corner by my bin.

So yes, I'm scared. . .

Scratch... Sniff... Grrrr...

Yikes, I can see it again! It's in the middle of the rug now. Whatever it is, it's really, horribly close!

"Your Majesty," I whisper. "There's something here, in my room." I comb my fingers through her soft fur.

"Hmm?" she asks sleepily.

"Your Majesty!" I hiss, shaking her gently. "Something's in my room!"

Sardine seems to notice what I'm saying or maybe she senses the creature herself because suddenly she pricks up her ears and bristles her fur.

Scratch... Sniff... Grrrr... HiSS!

Queen Sardine springs up onto her paws. "Mwooooooow. . . Who's there?" she howls, deep and low. I watch as she creeps to the edge of the bed, her body hunched and deadly fierce.

We wait.

We listen.

. . .

Silence.

. . .

"Who d'you think it is, Your Majesty?" I whisper.

"Shh!" she snaps. "Can't talk. Need to. . . smell."

Smell? I'll admit Queen Sardine does

smell a bit after she's eaten that icky fish
cat food she's so keen on, but I don't know
how smelling like an old trout

sniff

sniff

could help right now.

She wrinkles her nose
and sniffs once, twice,
three times. Oh gotcha
– she's trying to smell
the monster! Well, that
does make sense, I guess,
because Queen Sardine's a
great sniffer. All cats are, they have much
more powerful noses than we do. Not as
great as dogs, with their big wet sniffer-
dog snouts, but still pretty amazing.

She waves her nose in the air and takes one last deep breath. My heart's going BA-BOOM! BA-BOOM! in my chest, so hard and heavy I can almost hear it. I watch Sardine in the dim light, still crouched, watching the intruder. Then . . . with a tut and a groan, her whole body relaxes. "Molly! What on earth are you doing here? Ivy, for goodness' sake, turn on the light!"

Huh? Molly? The lovely big fluff-ball from the bungalow? She's one of the Kipper Street cats. There's lots of cats on my street, and they all love my best buddy, Queen Sardine. But why would

Molly be here in my room? And could she really have been making all those strange noises? I peel back my covers and reach for the lamp on my bedside table. Squinting in the bright light I scan my room.

My wastepaper bin's been knocked over. I binned a bunch of old felt-tip pens earlier today, and now they're all higgledy-piggledy across the floor, scattered by Miss Molly's

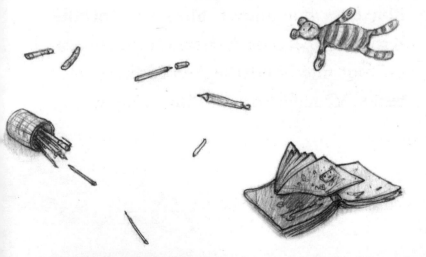

furry feet. But where is Molly?

"Down there," says Sardine, padding down the bed and leaning over. "Look, she's forgotten to hide her tail."

I lean over too, and quick as a flick Molly's tail disappears under my bed.

"Molly, it's okay," I say gently. "It's only us – Ivy and Queen Sardine." How can Molly be frightened of us?

I crawl out of my warm duvet and crouch down low to peer under the bed. "Please come out and tell us what's wrong." I can't see her, and to be honest, I'm not sure how she's even fitting under there. All my toys get shoved under my

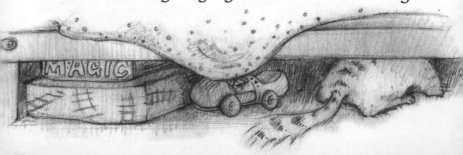

bed and there's not much room left for a big fluffy cat.

I can hear her mumbling in the darkness, though. "Nowhere safe…Nowhere good." She sounds a bit worried if you ask me. I wait, hoping she'll come out, but when she still doesn't appear, Queen Sardine jumps down to join me.

"There she is," she sighs. "There, between the keyboard and those silly shoes with wheels on."

My roller skates! They're not silly, but anyway. . . "I still can't see her. We can't all see in the dark, you know!" It's okay for Queen Sardine. She's got all these special night-time cat-senses.

"Oh yes," Her Majesty says. "Sometimes I forget you're only human. Sorry." She winks at me so I know she's only joking, then clears her throat with a sharp "meow", and puts her stern face on. "Molly, I order you to come out from under Miss Ivy's bed. This instant!"

Molly can't disobey her queen. Slowly a paw appears from the shadows, followed by another. Then a worried black-and-white stripy face pokes out. Molly used to seem so happy and cuddly, with her plush, plump cheeks, and her easy purr but now she's a frantic mess with wide eyes and matted fur.

"What's wrong?" Queen Sardine asks her.

Molly shakes her head to and fro. "Nowhere safe. . . Nowhere good. . ."

Her Majesty tuts and turns to me. "I don't know what's got into her! First she disappears for weeks on end. Then she shows up under your bed! I mean. . . oh! Where's she going now? Molly!"

But it's too late. Molly's waddled across my room, surprisingly fast, disappearing round the door. Seconds later we hear the

clip - clap

of the cat flap.

"Well!" says Queen Sardine. "That was peculiar."

With a dainty little wiggle of her stripy bottom, Sardine springs up onto my window sill and slips her head behind the curtain.

"There she goes – look. She's bumbling around in my front garden now!"

I join her at the window to see for myself. There's Molly over the road, sniffing about on the Trotts' doorstep and – oh. . . What's that?

Something much larger is shuffling up

the road away from our house. It's black and white, and as big as a dog. . .

"A badger?!" hisses Queen Sardine. "Oh, no. . . Badgers on Kipper Street? When did this happen?"

As I stroke Her Majesty's silky coat, I'm sure I feel her shudder. "I've heard horrible stories of badgers on Kipper Street, stories from long ago. But that old badger set's been empty for years!" she says. "Does this mean they're back? Back to rule the neighbourhood? I hear they bite, you know! With teeth as sharp as broken glass."

Queen Sardine stares, dazed, out of the

window then looks at me and gasps. "Do you suppose the badger scared Molly? I bet that's it! That must be why she's so scared. 'Nowhere safe,' she said. . . Molly was trying to find somewhere safe from the badger."

"No wonder she looked scared," I add. After all, I know what it's like to be scared of creatures in the dark.

Her Majesty is nodding her head and looking at me. She understands. "Molly's getting herself all worked up and silly in the head because the badgers are back on Kipper Street."

Cripes, badgers on Kipper Street! Okay

– yeah, I suppose Mum and Granny Mo might've mentioned something about there being a badger set at the bottom of the garden, but they said it was an *old* badger set! An underground set of homes that badgers hadn't lived in for years and years. Tunnels made by badgers of yesteryear and yore in ye olde Kipper Street days. Not real life modern-day badgers!

Our old badger set couldn't be back in use, could it? I'm sure we would have noticed badgers wandering up and down the garden. I bet the one we just saw outside is lost, or taking a stroll.

Queen Sardine droops her head and sighs. "I'm wide awake now. I think I'll nosy around the territory. Make sure the neighbourhood's in order."

Cats like to know who's where and what's what. And they're ultra-stressy about strangers showing up near their homes.

"Rest up, Ivy dear. I'll be back for breakfast," she says, and off she pitter-patters, out of my room and

clip - clap

out of the cat flap.

I hope she's safe out there in the dark with the badger!

I expect Her Majesty knows what she's doing, though, especially with all those supercat senses. Anyhow, it's not like I can go running around outside in the middle of the night making sure she's okay. Nope. All I can do is crawl back into bed and try not to think about nighttime nasties.

So I lie back down, pull my covers up over my shoulders, and stare at the ceiling. I stare and stare for what feels like forever, until finally the world fuzzes into sleepy darkness.

Kei's Plan

"We're going to camp!" Kei shrieks, tumbling into my room out of breath. "Your mum says you're allowed, and Granny Mo's says I'm allowed if you are, and—"

What time is it? When did Kei get here?

I love my mate Kei, don't get me wrong, but she's jumping up and down with excitement so much she's shaking the floorboards. I can tell she's on the verge of getting all "squeeeeeeee!" but I'm really tired. After all, I didn't get a whole lot of sleep last night.

Anyhow, I don't see what the big deal is. We've already camped in her room twice before – we put up Kei's tent and squashed it in between the bunk beds and the wardrobe. It was fun. Mostly. Can't say I really liked how dark it was in there, but other than that it was okay, I guess. We stayed up late, giggled lots, got told off for keeping everyone awake. It was kind of like a normal sleepover to be honest. So I don't get why Kei is so bouncy and squeaky about doing it a third time.

"Did you hear what I said, Ivy? We're going to properly camp! I've been at Granny Mo's since silly o'clock waiting to see you. Mum dropped me round hours ago, and I was going to come straight down but Mo said to wait, and I didn't *want* to wait but she said I had to and—"

"Woah. Slow down." I'm all sleepy and

Kei's speed-talking. By the way, Granny Mo isn't my actual gran, she's our upstairs neighbour, but I still call her that. She is Kei's granny, though, which is how we've become such good friends. Granny Mo is the opposite of Kei – calm and steady and thoughtful, whereas Kei always wants to jump headfirst into adventure. Which is one of the things I love about her. Usually.

Kei takes a deep breath and slows down just the teensiest bit. "Your mum let me in. She said to wake you up, that you've been dozing for ages. . . So come on, sleepy – let's test the tent in your garden! I've been waiting months and months and it's finally warm enough. Can you believe it!? We're actually going to sleep outside!"

No! Oh nonononono! No way! It's bad enough thinking 'bout the ghoulies and the vampires and the zombie brain-gobblers when I'm sleeping inside. I absolutely cannot sleep the night in a tent outside.

"Outside? In the garden?" I ask, clearly terrified.

Our garden is massive. It belongs to both flats, ours and Granny Mo's, so we all use it. There's a herb garden and a vegetable patch,

and loads of pretty potted plants. And in the daytime it's great for playing. There's a long lawn to run around on, and you can hide in the trees and bracken at the bottom. It's a lovely place. But I do not fancy spending a night out there!

When Kei sees my face her smile disappears. "You will, won't you? You'll camp with me – right, Ivy? I'm not allowed unless you're there too. Say you will?"

She looks so hopeful, her eyes wide and waiting, urging me to say yes.

I chew on my bottom lip while I try to think of the best way to let her down gently. "I'm sorry, Kei, but. . ."

"Please, please, please, please, pleeeeeeeeease. . ." she hisses under her breath in a desperate whisper.

Kei doesn't get it. She doesn't know how absolutely bone-jigglingly scared I get in the dark. And I'm too embarrassed to tell her. I mean, how many eight-year-olds still worry about monsters? Kei is fearless. Never in a squillion years would she be fretting over imaginary ghosts 'n' ghouls. No way can I tell her how I feel!

"Okay," I mumble. And honestly, how oh how am I agreeing to this? I must be crazy.

"You mean it, you will?" she asks, looking really keen and excited again.

I nod. Yup, crazy.

"WOOHOO!" screams Kei. Then, before I can blink, she's out of the door, running down the hall, shouting as she goes. "Come on, Ivy, we're gonna have so much fun!"

Once I've hauled myself out of bed, and into my dressing gown and slippers, I find Kei in the garden with Queen Sardine.

Phew! Her Majesty's safe and sound.

She purrs loudly when she sees me and slinks over to my side. "Your friend's been busy," she says, and she's not wrong.

Kei's grinning, rocking on her heels, pointing down the garden at her tent.

"Oh," I say. "That was quick." I try to sound impressed but what I'm really thinking is, isn't that a bit far to walk in the dark if I suddenly need to pee? And, when exactly did we say we were going to do this camping thing anyway?

"Well, yeah. Been practising, haven't I?"

Kei runs up to me, gives me a hug, then dashes inside yelling, "Sleeping bags!"

Oh please tell me we're not doing this tonight?

"Why are you looking so glum?" Sardine asks.

I flop down next to her feeling babyish and sulky. "It's the camping," I tell her. "I'm scared of the dark." And *ping!* there it is: the truth. I can't tell Kei, but I have to tell someone, and maybe – just maybe – Sardine will be able to help.

Queen Sardine frowns. "Then why did you agree to do it if—"

"You saw how excited Kei was," I explain.

Sardine nestles into the space under

my knees. "You didn't want to disappoint her," she says, and she goes very still and quiet, like she's thinking hard. "You didn't disappoint her, and I won't disappoint you!" she announces.

"But how?"

"I'll protect you!" she says. "From these

night-time nasties you're worrying about. I'll be your watch-cat! Just please don't tell anyone. I can't have the Kipper Street cats thinking their queen's doing doggy duties."

Now, I've no flipping clue if Sardine could actually protect me from anything, but oh, I love love love that she wants to! And I know I'll feel safer sleeping outside if Her Majesty is with me. She really is the best friend ever.

"You mean..."

"I mean," she says, "I'll keep watch while you're sleeping. I'll be just outside the tent. And if anything creepy or ghoulish shows up, then I'll get my claws out and show it who's boss! But, Ivy...this stuff is always worse in your imagination, you know. I bet you a fish supper you'll look back afterwards and wonder what on earth you were worried about."

I still feel nervous but I like that Sardine's trying to make me feel better. And it's working. It might not sound like much, having a cat guard your tent, but now I'm grinning ear to ear. With Queen Sardine there I think maybe – just maybe – I can do this camping thing without lying awake terrified all night.

But then I remember. "You can't hang about in the garden all night! What if that badger comes back? What if he's dangerous?"

I'm certain I see her shudder but she shakes her head all the same. "I expect badgers are only dangerous if you let them think they're in charge. If he comes back, I'll let him know who's boss. I'll be. . . absolutely fine."

She doesn't sound too sure about that.

"But you said. . . you heard stories—" I start.

"What I said," says my brave and best ever buddy, "Is that

36

I'll protect you, Ivy Meadows."
And with that, Her Majesty crawls out
from under my legs, finds a sunny patch
of grass, and sprawls out.

"What if the badger. . ." I start to say,
but Queen Sardine does this loud, over-
the-top fake yawn, and I know she isn't
listening.

She closes her eyes and firmly says, "Shush, now. . . No more talking. It's catnap time." Which sounds kind of rude, but really it's not. Really she's shushing me cos she wants to help with my fear of the dark. Even if that means facing up to her fear too.

Because, let's face it, badgers don't exactly sound like snuggly little teddy bears, do they? Queen Sardine is scared of them, and I don't blame her.

A KIPPER ST KERFUFFLE

Well, the tent's up, like I said, and we've been down to the shops with Mum to get some "just-this-once" snacks for our midnight feast (which is another one of Kei's ideas, but one I'm really liking).

I'm starting to think we might not fit in the tent once all the biscuits and buns and bananas and stuff are in there.

Still, at least we'll have plenty of spare grub to chuck at monsters. Or badgers. Or monster-badgers. You know. . . just in case.

Anyway, me, Mum and Kei are trudging back down Kipper Street with our shopping bags when I spot a stripy tail disappearing under our garden gate. Not a gingery tabby-cat tail like Queen Sardine's. This tail is black and white and grey, and if I'm not mistaken it belongs to. . .

"Molly! Molly, wait!" Benny the stray bounds past us, jumping the fence into our front garden. "Where'd she go?" I hear him grumble as Mum unlatches the gate.

Something weird is going on.

"Oh look, Benny's in our garden again," says Mum. "Do you think he's looking for Queen Sardine?"

Benny's ears prick up at Her Majesty's name. "Is she here?" he asks me, turning to face us.

"How sweet!" trills Kei. "It's like he's talking to us!"

And of course he is talking to us, but I'm the only one who can understand him! Still, I can't exactly explain that to Mum and Kei, can I? They'd think I was bonkers.

So I lag behind as they carry the bags up the front path, then into the house. I need a quick chat with Benny.

"Where is she, Miss Ivy? I need 'er

42

Majesty!" His eyes scan the garden as he talks.

"What's wrong, Sir Benny? What's happening?" I ask, just before a gang of Kipper Street cats spring onto our garden fence. They balance on the wooden slats in a wobbly line, scrabbling to stay upright as they yowl for Benny's attention.

"Oh flippin' whiskers," groans Benny.

And then all of the cats start complaining at once. . .

"Meow! She's done it again!"

"Sir Benny, you have to do something!"

"I found her in my people's shed."

"I found her on my people's bed!"

"She ate my brekky!"

"She gobbled my treats!"

"Sir Benny! Sir Benny! Sir Benny!" they chorus, wailing.

"Who are they talking about?" I whisper to Benny. "Not Queen Sardine?" Her Majesty can sometimes rub people up the wrong way, but I can't imagine her stealing other cats' food. Unless it was her favourite fish, sardines. Oh dear.

Benny shakes his furry head, "No, of course not, not Her Highness. It's Molly. They want me to do something about Molly," he whispers back.

Oh. Molly, again?

"She's sneaking into our homes and noshing on our food!" whines Whiskers.

"She's sniffing round all our comfy hideouts. I went to rclax in my usual spot behind my people's shed this morning, and who'd got there first? Molly!"

"But why? She's never behaved like this before, has she?" I ask.

The cats mewl and meowl and shrug,

staring at Benny with demanding eyes.

"Sir Benny," shrills Sprout, "It's your job to protect us. You must do something!"

Benny's mouth opens and closes but I don't think he knows what to say. He looks confused. Balancing my shopping bags I snatch him up into my arms, and usher the other cats away. "Sir Benny needs some peace and quiet to think. Off you go!" I tell them. And when they don't leave, I carry Benny inside with me and close the door.

Phew. Poor Sir Benny. He's Queen Sardine's very own knight, so all the Kipper Street cats ask him for help before bothering Her Majesty. But how do they expect him to magically fix this? It sounds like things are getting serious. We need to track down Molly and talk to her, but first we need to find Queen Sardine.

"Her Majesty's probably still sunning herself out back," I tell Benny as I set him down in the hallway.

"Come on, then!" he shouts, bounding off. We scurry through the hall to the kitchen, where Kei and Mum are unpacking the shopping.

Benny's a blur as he dashes past them

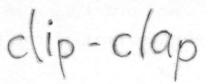

and out through the cat flap.

"I'll just be a minute!" I call to Mum

and Kei, who are still pulling goodies from the shopping bags, and I race out of the back door.

I was right. Queen Sardine hasn't moved since this morning. She's where I left her, on the patio. But now she's up on all fours, focused, listening. She stares at something down the garden. Her ears twitch as if she can hear something I can't.

"Ahem!" coughs Benny to get her attention. "Your Majesty. . ."

"Shhh, I'm watching the tent," whispers Sardinc.

Weird. Maybe she's got confused about this watch-cat idea.

"Your Majesty," I explain, "you don't need to guard the tent till I'm actually in it."

But Her Royal Highness only tuts and keeps her half-open eyes fixed on the tent.

"Er. . . Benny's here, Your Majesty. He needs your help. It's Molly – she's behaving strangely again and causing all sorts of mayhem. The Kipper Street cats are in a tizz about it, but we don't know what to do!"

"I can see that," she whispers. "Keep your voice down."

"Why?" I ask, confused.

"Shh!" she hisses. "You'll scare

her away!"

"Who?" Benny and I ask at the same time. We look around the garden. There's no one here.

"Molly, of course," sighs Her Majesty. "She's in the tent," she says, shaking the patio-dust off her silky coat. "I suppose it's time she and I had a little word."

Benny and I look at each other and smile. We've tracked down Molly, and Queen Sardine has a plan. What a relief!

"Claws 'n' catnip," whispers Benny, grinning and shaking his head "You really are a wondercat, Your Majesty."

MOLLY'S TUM

When we reach the tent, Benny and I hover at the zip-up tent door and Her Majesty slinks inside.

Hiss!

"Now, now, Molly! You're addressing your queen, remember. None of that hissing nonsense. It's time to sit down and tell me what's going on. Though I must say, from the look of you, I've got an idea. . ."

I can't resist poking my head inside the tent to see what Sardine means, and Benny does the same. Molly flinches back, and Queen Sardine shoos us out again, but I think I noticed something different about Molly. . .

"Her tummy's enormous!" Benny gasps. I was too polite to say anything, but. . ."Must be all those dinners she's been gobblin'. Gone straight to her middle, eh? Well I never!"

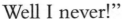

"But why?" I whisper back.

A low moan comes from Molly, inside the tent, followed by those same words she kept saying last night: "Nowhere safe."

And when I hear Queen Sardine speak next, her voice is oh so gentle. "Molly, I want to help you. Won't you just talk about it?"

"There's nothing to talk about!"

"Now, Molly, there's plenty to talk about but nothing to worry about. Why don't I take you home, back to your lovely owners at the bungalow? We can talk on the way. . ."

"No!" hisses Molly. "Nowhere safe!"

Then she takes us by surprise, shoving through the tent door, knocking us sideways, and wobbling off down the lawn.

We chase her but when I catch up with Molly (she's not exactly fast) I'm not sure what to do. I mean, she might lash out if I try to grab her, and I don't want to make the situation worse. Benny and I beg her to wait but of course she doesn't, and when I look back for Queen Sardine, I see that my furry friend is all tangled up in the tent strings.

"Your Majesty!" mewls Benny, running back to help her.

But Sardine's gaze is fixed on Molly, who is now quite far away.

"Molly! Miss Molly Mopsy Malone!" she screeches. "It's all going to be fine! You're not the first cat to have…" Sardine's voice trails off. "Kittens." She sighs. Molly's much too far away to hear Her Majesty now.

But I heard! Oh boy, did I hear! Kittens. KITTENS. K-i-t-t-e-n-s! That beautiful, cute-iful, loveliest of words ever.

"Kittens! Are you sure?" I gush, trying to untangle Sardine without snagging her fur. "But. . . How can you tell?"

Sardine shakes her ruffled coat, smiling all the while. "A queen knows these things, my dear girl. The eating, the looking for shelter, the expansive tummy – they're all telltale signs." She licks her paws, then sits back, poised once again. Thinking.

"Poor Molly," she says. "Carrying kittens can be a confusing time. Instincts

take over. All this stuff about nowhere being safe…she's clearly got her whiskers twisted trying to find just the right spot to have the kits. Somewhere warm. Somewhere calm. Though why oh why doesn't she want to have her babies at the bungalow? Surely her people want to look after her?"

Molly's owners are quiet stay-indoorsy-type people. They are sisters, but older than Mum, with pretty red hair. I don't see them much, and they never say more than "hello" when I do see them. They always smile though.

Suddenly Queen Sardine gasps and

stares at me. "Oh, hairballs!" she says. "What if her people don't know? Ivy, you have to speak with them! We have to be certain they know what's happening."

I nod frantically. We absolutely must make sure Molly's owners know that she is pregnant. Their cat needs extra-special looking after right now. I try to act natural when the back door swings open and Kei races out to join me.

"Molly's having kittens!" I blurt out.

"Kittens? Yay!" she squeals. Suddenly Kei looks confused. "Who's Molly?"

When I describe the big, stripy, loveable black-and-white moggy, Kei squeals again at the thought of black-and-white stripy kittens. Meanwhile Queen Sardine and Benny are staring at me, urging me into action. I can't talk to them in front of Kei, though, she'd think I was mad!

"We have to tell Molly's owners," I say. Sardine's jaw drops – she certainly doesn't think anybody "owns" her! – but I keep my attention on Kei. "I don't know them well. I know where they live, but we can't just knock on their door, can we?"

But Kei's pulling me by the hands. "Yes we can, let's go!"

I stumble forward as she yanks me up. "Wait! Just wait a second, okay? We don't know Molly's owners. They look nice enough, but – hey – they could be witches or werewolves or goblins for all we know!"

Kei rolls her eyes, but then she flashes a big toothy grin. "It's fine," she says. "We'll take Granny Mo."

So off we fly to the flat upstairs from mine, where Granny Mo is sipping on milky coffee and listening to her radio. By the time we get there we're totally puffed out and can only manage to talk in broken sentences.

"Got to," I wheeze.

"Come quick," gasps Kei.

"Molly—"

"Tummy full of . . ."

"KITTENS!" we shout together.

"Please help, got to—"

"Tell her owners—"

"She, lives at. . ."

"The bungalow. Yes, I know Molly," says Granny Mo. "Though, to be honest, I'm surprised she's back on Kipper Street. . . Oh dear. No, little ladies, this is not good. Not good at all. . ." She scratches her head and paces to the window.

Granny Mo's brow has a deep crease in it, which means she's worried.

"What is it?" asks Kei, looking all frowny and panicked. "Granny, what's wrong?"

Granny Mo suddenly looks ready for action. She grabs her purse and keys, and ushers us to the door. "What's wrong," she explains, "is that Molly's people moved out months ago." She wriggles her feet into a pair of sandals while my mind turns her words over and over again like a pancake that just will not cook.

Because she can't be saying what I think she's saying. Can she?

"They've left Kipper Street? Her owners have gone. . . Just like that?" I ask. I feel breathless again but this time it's not from running upstairs.

Granny Mo nods. "Uh-huh. And they took Molly with them! She must've walked 'cross all of Squiddly to get back here. I'll ask around, see if I can get their new address. It might take some time to track them down. For now, let's focus on findin' that cat and gettin' her inside, somewhere safe. We'll try the bungalow first."

Kei looks back up at me as we head downstairs, pausing to say the same words I'm thinking: "Molly's all alone."

"Yeah," I sigh.

Then I pull myself together. Molly is alone for now, but hopefully not for long. We'll help the silly cat!

If we can find her.

KIPPER STREET

Moments later, we're standing outside the bungalow at the end of Kipper Street – me, Kei, Granny Mo and Mum (who we picked up on the way because, let's face it, this is serious!).

Granny Mo was right: Molly's old home is empty. The blinds are pulled right up and there's no furniture inside. Plus there's a SOLD sign in the garden that I didn't notice before.

Molly might be feeling confused, but she is right about one thing, she really hasn't got anywhere safe to call home on Kipper Street. The bungalow is all locked up.

"We've got to find that poor cat, Mo," sighs Mum, still staring at the empty bungalow. "The poor thing. All alone without a home."

"She does have a home," Kei says. "But it's somewhere on the other side of Squiddly!"

"Cats don't always see things the way we do," Mum says, and I know she's right. "It takes them a while to see a new house as theirs. I suppose this bungalow on Kipper Street felt like her real home, but when she got back here everything was dark and empty and different. No wonder she's scared."

Granny Mo wraps one arm around Mum's shoulders and the other around me and Kei. "Don't worry," she says, comforting us. "Molly needs a place to stay, all right, somewhere to have dem kittens. Well, I got jus' the place in mind."

WRONG

We looked for Molly all day, Kei and me. We even made some leaflets on the computer and spent the afternoon posting them through people's doors, sticking them on lampposts, sliding them under windscreen wipers on cars. But still no one's phoned to say they've found her, and it's gone eight o'clock.

Mum says that Molly's bound to turn

up tomorrow, and I hope she's right. But now it's getting late – we've eaten pizza for dinner, brushed our teeth ready for bed, and have said nighty-night to Mum and Granny Mo.

I can't ignore it any longer. It's time to go camping in the garden. My first outside sleepover. Eek!

"Remember, Ivy, I'll be right outside,

keeping watch the whole time. There's nothing to worry about," says Queen Sardine, wrapping herself round my ankles as I stand in front of Kei's tent.

Kei, of course, is already inside, sorting out the food for our not-so-secret midnight feast.

Sighing, I crouch down low and give Her Majesty a thank-you tickle, behind

her ears where she likes it most. Then I whisper goodnight and crawl inside.

The tent smells plasticky. It's warmer inside than I was expecting and the sun is low in the sky, lighting up the space with a soft orange glow. Our sleeping

bags, pillows and blankets are neatly arranged side by side, and our snacks are stacked in the middle of the floor, ready for gobbling. It all looks, well... pretty wonderful if I'm honest!

I can see why Kei's been so excited to camp for so long. This is fun! It's like having your own little house with all your own rules. Or, I should say, with no rules at all! Because we can sing crazy-loud, we can stuff our cheeks up with marshmallows, we can gargle with lemonade. It's heaven.

We eat until we're nearly bursting and the tent floor's dotted with biscuit crumbs, and then we laugh until we can barely

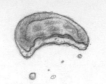

breathe. Eventually we cosy down into our sleeping bags, grinning.

Kei's so happy and I suddenly realise I'm happy too! I was petrified before, but this really is the most, hilari-tastic, fantasti-fun time I've ever ever had!

Until Kei pulls two big torches out from behind her back. "Might need these soon," she says, passing me one.

She's right. Soon the sun will set with one last splash of pink and gold, and then that'll be it. Darkness.

This is the scary bit. The bone-quaking shiversome bit. The surviving a whole night outside bit. The managing not to get eaten by a bloodthirsty snot demon bit. This is the part of the evening I've been dreading, where day turns to night. And here's Kei, grinning like it's Christmas.

"I was going to wait till later to tell ghost stories, but I can't wait, can you?" she asks excitedly. I'm so nervous now I want leave the tent and run inside.

"No ghost stories!" I tell her. "I mean it. Nothing too scary, or you're on your own out here." And by "nothing too scary" I mean "nothing at all scary", but I don't want to sound like a total wimp in front of Kei.

"Don't worry, silly," Kei trills. "It's a funny ghost story, not a scary one. Funny's okay, right?"

I raise an eyebrow at her. Kei's idea of "not scary" might not fit with mine.

"Good," she says, "Get comfy, then. This story's about the headless owl of Kipper Street."

"Too scary," I groan, but Kei shakes her head and insists that, no, this headless owl tale is giggle-full and scare-free. Hmph. Well, I guess we'll see. . .

"There was this owl. . ." she begins. "An owl who all the Kipper Street birds were jealous of. Cos the thing about owls, right, is that they can turn their heads all the way round so they're back to front. Well, that's exactly what the Kipper Street owl used to do, but the other birds couldn't turn their heads like that, so they got all huffy. And cos owls are nocturnal, the Kipper Street owl didn't even know the other birds were jealous. They did all their grumbling and moaning in the daytime, see, when the owl was sleeping. And that's also when they hatched their evil plan."

Kei cackles then scrunches her nose up, pulling her "evil-genius" face. Then she makes beaks with her hands and pretends to make them whisper to each other. I can't pretend it's not funny, but I'm a bit edgy right now. . . and Kei's evil birdies feel scarier than they probably should.

"One morning," she says, "when the owl was dozing, the birds flocked together and zoomed round and round her, tweeting and squawking like anything. They woke up the Kipper Street owl, and she was miffed! She kept twisting her neck round and round, trying to see who was disturbing her. But the flock of birds kept

flying round and round her, faster and faster. So round and round she turned her head, twisting her neck, until. . . SNAP! Her head fell off!"

Kei claps her hands for effect – yeesh! – then sits back looking terribly serious and wide-eyed. "And ever since," she continues, "the ghost of the Kipper Street owl has been searching for the birds that made her head fall off. Calling –" she cups her hands together and holds them to her mouth – "Whooooooooooooo?"

She keeps repeating it in this funny owl-voice and when I start giggling, Kei leans in close to me singing, "Yooooouuuuuuuu!

It was yooooouuuuuuu!" Then she does a mini bow and says, "See – I told you it was funny."

But you see, right now it *is* funny. Right now it's headless hoots aplenty. But I know that later the idea of a headless owl will start to seem a bit less ha-ha. . . and a bit more yikes.

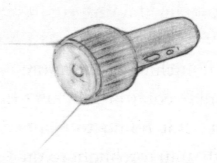

KITTENS

It's black outside now. We can't see without the torches. Kei and I have already demolished the crisps and popcorn, and we're halfway through a packet of Jaffa Cakes. We're both agreed that we need to stop munching now, before we're sick. We should really brush our teeth again, but that's not going to happen tonight. Not with only torchlight to guide us back indoors. So we stuff our leftovers into a backpack, dump it in the doorway by our shoes, then bury ourselves deep inside our snuggly sleeping bags.

Kei's brain must have an on/off switch. Within minutes of lying down and closing her eyes she's zonked out, fast asleep. Whereas I'm wide awake, shivering and quaking with fear.

I can't stop thinking about the headless owl of Kipper Street.

It's not even real, I tell myself. Though the sounds of branches creaking and leaves rustling in the trees don't do much to convince me. And when an owl – no joke – decides to *hooooot* right above the tent, I almost grab my torch and run inside. But that would mean going outside in the dark. If I ran, the headless owl would most definitely get me. Oh crackers. Oh crumbs!

This is going to be a very long night.

"Ivy, is that you shuffling about in there?"

I squeal in surprise, but I know that voice. It's Her Majesty. Queen Sardine is guarding our tent, being our watch-cat just like she promised.

"I can't sleep," I whisper back.

"Try closing your eyes," she says. "I'll be right here the whole time. I excel in all I do, young Ivy. And what I'm doing now," she says, then drops her voice to a whisper like she's worried someone might overhear her, "is keeping you totally and utterly safe!"

And actually, knowing she's there does make me feel safe. At least, safe enough that my heart stops hammering.

I close my eyes and soon enough, I find myself relaxing.

I could almost be in my bedroom, with Queen Sardine right there at my side. Keeping me safe and warm, as I finally start. . . to. . . drift. . .

Squeeeaaak! Eeeep! Peeeep peeeep!

Huh? What's happening? Where am I?

"Ivy, quick! Wake up! That sounds like kittens!"

Queen Sardine? How did she get in here? "Your Majesty. . . When did you...?"

I rub the sleep from my eyes and try to look around in the dark tent.

She sighs. "Those troublesome badgers were scuffling around."

Eep – the badgers! I'd forgotten all about them. With all the Molly-panic I didn't even tell Mum. Are badgers really here, in our back garden? Right now?

"I called for you, but you were out cold," says Sardine. "Your friend Kei let me in. Fell straight back asleep afterwards, mind you."

I look at Kei, her eyes shut, her mouth gaping open.

"Oh," I say, sitting up.

"I was still guarding you, you understand. From inside…"

"Yes. Thanks. Okay. Kittens? Oh. Oh. They're here? The kittens are here? Here in my garden?"

Meeeep! Squeeaak… meep!

Queen Sardine pulls a slightly impatient well-what-do-you-think face?

All fears of headless owls and night-time ghouls aside, I need to see these kittens! But before I've had a chance to track down a torch and pull on a jumper, we hear another sound. An awful sound.

Yoooooooooow//

"It's Molly!" hisses Queen Sardine. "Something's wrong! Quick!"

Her Majesty disappears from the tent. There's no time to find my torch. No time to pull on my shoes. Molly and the kittens could be in danger.

It seems wrong to leave Kei all alone. I jiggle her shoulder to see how deeply she's sleeping but she doesn't move.

"Kei? You awake?" I whisper, which is a totally daft question.

She is fast asleep.

So, leaving Kei, I head out into the night.

My feet squelch on the dewy grass and my eyes do their best to adjust to the darkness as I follow my ears towards the sounds of mum-cat and kittens.

Yowl! Peeep!

"Here, Ivy. Here by the drain," Her Majesty calls to me, and suddenly I see them all. A black-and-white mess of paws, fur and whiskers. Lovely, stripy Molly, and three wriggling kits. Adorable!

Their eyes are all tight shut as they wobble and tumble around their mum. They don't even really look like kittens yet. More like soft little moles, all wrinkled and lovely. And I suddenly realise I'm standing outside, in the dark, being brilliantly brave, without even knowing

it! I really could stay here all night just watching these peeping-meeping little babies.

But something's wrong with Molly. She keeps nudging the kittens with her nose and counting, "One, two, three. . . One, two, three. . ."

"What's wrong?" I ask. "What is it?"

Queen Sardine shakes her head. She's as confused as I am.

Then Molly stops counting and starts yowling again. "Four!" she cries. "There were four!"

LORD SNIFFSALOT

Leaving Molly to care for kittens one, two and three, we set out to search for kitten number four. Queen Sardine sniffs about the garden with her super-sniffer powers as we search through marigold beds, under broken plant pots, behind the spiderwebby shed. . .

Where is this kitten?!

Queen Sardine grimaces and bops

herself hard on the nose. "It's no good!" she sighs. "There are too many smells out here. My silly nose can't find the kitten among all the other pongs. This garden honks of foxes. Badgers too. Not to mention every cat in Kipper Street who's decided to visit your garden."

"It's okay, Your Majesty, we'll just search with our eyes," I say. And we do. Mine have adjusted to the dark now and Sardine's got supercat vision. We look everywhere!

Well, almost everywhere. After we've peered behind every bush and pot we still haven't seen any sight of the lost kitten.

But there's one place we haven't looked yet — the badger sets at the bottom of the garden.

"You don't think. . . The kitten couldn't have. . ." I stammer, not quite able to say the words.

"Tumbled into a badger set?" murmurs Queen Sardine. "Maybe." She closes her eyes for a moment, breathes deeply, and hesitates. She turns to me and whispers, "Ivy, I'm. . . scared."

Queen Sardine looks so embarrassed. Her head is hanging low and her eyes won't meet mine.

"It's okay," I say. "It's okay to be scared.

You helped me, and I'll help you." I tickle her head, hoping my friend will perk up. "It's like you said, Your Majesty. This stuff is always worse in your imagination. I was terrified of camping. I really was! But. . . it's actually been kind of fun. And maybe the badgers will turn out the same!"

Queen Sardine raises an eyebrow in disbelief, but still stares at the ground.

"Maybe they won't be as bad as you think," I tell her. "Maybe they won't really have teeth like broken glass. Maybe they'll be. . . okay. And if they're not okay, well, we'll deal with them together."

"We will?" she whispers, daring to look

at me now. "You'll come with me?"

Is she serious? I'm hardly going to leave my best friend to do this on her own, am I? "Of course, sill— I mean, Your Majesty."

She stands taller now, fixing me with her big green eyes. "Thank you, Ivy! Oh thank you, thank you!" she says in a whispered flurry. "We'll do this together. Right. . ."

And with a quick shake of her whiskers, Queen Sardine bounds down to the bottom of the garden. Right down to the really spooky space with tall trees and overgrown bushes. And I clamber behind her, barefoot.

The mouth of the badger set is draped in ivy (the plant, not me) so it's hard to see it until you're quite close, gaping at the hole which leads down underground to where the badgers sleep. Queen Sardine stands in front of the set, nods to herself, then calls in.

"Hello? Badgers?" The words echo down the damp, mud tunnel.

And when no one replies, Her Majesty starts muttering to herself, like she's building up to doing something. But what? "Worse in my imagination. Not as bad as I think."

Then, before I can stop her, she plunges into the hole! And quickly I do something which you should never do to cats. And I mean never ever — not unless you want to lose a hand and a friend all in one go.

This is what I do: I reach in after Queen Sardine, grab her tail, and pull her back out again.

Mrrrrooooooool! Hissss!

Queen Sardine looks at me like I've lost my mind. Her ears flatten and her fur spikes.

But I had to do it, I had to! It's for her own good. She can't just throw herself down the badger set. "You can't go in, Your Majesty, they might hurt you! Even if they *are* okay, the badgers won't want you to go marching in there!" I say.

"But the kitten!" she pants, breathless. "We have to save that kitten."

"Please! You can't help the kitten if you're hurt, though, can you? You're a queen. And this is your garden, your territory."

Queen Sardine turns back to me, her face suddenly thoughtful. "My territory. . ." she mutters. "Yes. Yes, Ivy,

99

I think perhaps you're right."

She clears her throat, leans into the hole and calls, "Badgers! The Queen of the Kipper Street cats and ruler of this garden demands to meet with you! Come out and talk with me."

She sits back, staring into silence, waiting for a response. But there is no reply. Maybe this is just an old badger set and they aren't living here after all. A minute or so passes and she tries again, a tad less queenly this time. "Ahem! Badgers! You brutish bullies had better get your big, furry backsides out here now, or else!"

"Or else what?" rumbles a deep earthy voice from behind us.

Gulp.

We both spin round, and together we take a sharp, uneasy breath. Cos standing on its huge back legs, looming over us, is the most enormous badger! And – even more of a shocker – I can understand him!

"I said, 'or else what?'" he growls.

Her Majesty hisses at me, "Get back, Ivy!" Then she sandwiches herself between me and the badger. I can tell she's scared. Her fur is all bristly and she's trembling. Even so, she stands her ground

– my best friend is so brave!

"Or else," she says, "I'm going into your set!"

"NOT ON YOUR WHISKERS!" the badger roars, lurching forward and baring his sharp, glistening teeth.

Oh no, no, no, no! He looks crazy. Brutal and grizzly and crazy. We've got to run. Got to get away. But as I turn my head to choose an escape route, I realise just how much trouble we're in. Cos all around us in the dark are pairs of eyes, staring right at me and Sardine. Eyes belonging to big, angry badgers.

"Your Majesty!" I gasp. "They're everywhere!"

The big badger chuckles. I guess he can understand me too.

A small hiss escapes Queen Sardine but she steadies herself, facing the crazy badger-bully. "Now listen, you!" she says. "There's a chance a kitten might be stuck down that hole of yours. And I don't give two hoots how scary you think you are – I'm going to find it! Now, you can help me or not. Either way, I've got a job to do!"

103

"A KITTEN!" yells the badger, then pauses. "A kitten, eh?"

All around us, the badgers are murmuring.

"Hmm, a lost kitten, y'say. Well, that's a different matter!"

Her Majesty looks back at me, her brow knotted in confusion.

"Er, excuse me, Mr Badger, sir," I stammer. "Is there any ch-chance you could. . . h-help us?"

He sniffs, coughs, and mutters to himself. "Guess I'll have to," he says. "Can't exactly leave a kitten on its own a' this time o'night."

He looks round at the other badgers to let them know his mind's made up. He's clearly in charge here, the chief badger. "Yes, we'll help. We'll track down that little' un of yours. Got superior sniffers, don't we?" he says, tapping his nose with his paw.

The other badgers roar with laughter, and Queen Sardine ignores the insult.

"Well... thank you," says Her Majesty. "Right then. Should I follow you down there?" She doesn't sound too keen on the idea, but

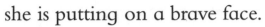

she is putting on a brave face.

The chief badger sniffs round the opening to the set. "Nah," he says. "No kittens 'ere." He shouts to the others, "Gerrinside, boys! This won't take long." And as the other badgers vanish into the hole one black-and-white bottom at a time, he turns to us. "If there's one thing Lord Sniffsalot is good at, it's trackin'. Now ge' behind me, 'n' try to keep up!"

Her Majesty and I glance at each other, shrug, then stand in a funny little queue behind him.

"Are, er, you Lord Sniffsalot?" I ask as he leads the way, nose first.

"Wha' d'you think, Miss Jaffa Cakes?" he mutters.

Woah. He can smell the crumbs on me? That's quite some nose. If anyone can find these kittens, surely Sir Sniffsalot can!

With a quick sniff of the air our guide gets wind of something. "This way," he snuffles, and putting all our faith in this grumpy badger, we cross our fingers and paws, and follow.

THE FOURTH KITTEN

"Don't panic, Molly!" Queen Sardine calls. Lord Sniffsalot is leading us closer and closer to where she is huddled with her kittens. "The badger's here to help us find your kitten. He just needs to, er, sniff you all. Just quickly. He won't get too close, will you, Lord Sniffsalot?"

sniff

The big badger snorts. "Nah. No need. I can smell the kits from 'ere!"

Molly scowls, standing over her kittens like a fierce tigress. She is very protective of her new babies, but she nods.

Waving his nose in the cool night air, Lord Sniffsalot closes his eyes and sniffs. "Yeah, s'what I thought," he says.

"What?" gasps Queen Sardine. "What is it?"

"Tha' smell," he says. "The little 'uns 'ave got a pong, see. Subtle it is, but a nose like mine'll catch it, no problem."

"Well, that's good, isn't it?" I ask. "That means you'll be able to track down the

fourth kitten?"

"Done it already, Miss Jaffa Cakes. Caught a scent of something similar just over the way there." He flicks his nose towards Granny Mo's herb patch. "Just wanted to be sure before investigating. You cats is nervous things. If I got it wrong 'n' stumbled on a sleeping mog, it'd prob'ly yowl the 'ole street down complainin'!"

Queen Sardine rolls her eyes but it seems to me that both the badgers and the cats might have some wrong ideas about each other.

"Well, what are we waiting for, then? Lead the way," she says.

"Let's see," he says. "What am I waiting for… Well, firstly, 'ow's about an apology?" He glares at Her Majesty, who takes a brisk step back, bumping into my ankles.

"For what?" she yelps. "You'd have me grovelling to you, while a tiny kitten's all alone somewhere? Why you. . . big bullying brute!"

Lord Sniffsalot laughs a snarly laugh, "You'll apologise for bad-mouthing me 'n' all my buddies. Big we may be. Grumpy sometimes, I'll give y' that. But bullies? Nah. And if y' want our kind to gerralong wi' your kind, then you'll be wise to say 'sorry'. "

"Well!" gasps Her Majesty.

Lord Sniffsalot sits back on his hind legs, a smug half-smile growing on his face. "Take your time wi' that apology," he says. "I can wait."

A soft growl rumbles from Queen Sardine, but she pushes it back down, grits her teeth and says, "Lord Sniffsalot, on behalf of myself and of all the cats who have ever lived ever, I humbly and graciously apologise for any bad-mouthing that may have offended you or your kind."

I wince. There's no missing the sarcasm

dripping from Her Majesty's words. I wait for Lord Sniffsalot's angry reaction, but he just chuckles! Either he can't hear the sarcasm or he doesn't care.

"Right y'are, then!" he says. "Let's be findin' the kit!"

We follow him just ten steps and he stops. "There!" he says. "Was never in any danger. Little scamp musta stumbled into the basil, gotten cosy 'n' fallen straight to sleep. 'Ere, look at 'im, he's an 'ansome chap. Wi' those markin's he could almost be a badger pup!"

"Him? He's a he?" I ask.

Lord Sniffsalot nods proudly. "Hiding his pong among the basil like that – a lesser nose would'a missed 'im!" he chuckles. And he's right! What would we have done without his "superior sniffer"?

When I peer into Granny Mo's herbs, I see him. The lost-and-found kitten. A tiny

ball of white-and-black skin, with eyes
shut tight, sleeping soundly in the thick,
bushy basil.

"Is. . . Is it safe for me to pick him up?"
I ask Queen Sardine.

Her Majesty is staring at the little baby bundle with a gooey, happy look on her face. "Yes. Gently, gently," she coos as I cup my hands around the kitten and pull him close for warmth.

He's so tiny, so light, so new and precious that it's hard to believe he managed to wander off on his own!

And, oh! As I lift him close to my chest I feel him stretch and shudder and then...

Meep! Peep! Meeew!

He's awake! The kitten is pushing his teeny, warm little head against my fingers.

And I think I might melt into a pool of mushiness because this is absolutely the cutest thing ever.

"Thank you," says Queen Sardine to our badger guide, and she sounds like she really means it. Let's face it, without him we might never have found kitten number four.

"Nah. Don't mention it," he says. "You know I would've led you to 'im with or without the apology, right?" He winks and starts to amble back down the garden, calling over his shoulder, "But I've got your word now, int' I? No more peeing round the set!" And with that he disappears down that not-so-scary-after-all hole.

I place the delicate baby cat ever so carefully down on his mum, who cries and purrs all at once.

"My little one! Oh, thank you. Thank you!" Molly splutters, and she licks and nuzzles the little kitten. "He. . . oh!" she exclaims. "He tastes of basil!"

She looks confused but shrugs and goes back to licking him clean.

And that's when it strikes me. "Basil!" I say.

"Yes?" say Her Majesty and Molly.

"Basil! It's a name!" I tell them.

"Yes," says Molly, nodding. "Yes, Basil's a good name. A very good name. Basil. This one's called Basil. Oh, thank you, Ivy, I think I might let you name the others," she says with a lazy smile.

I get to name the kittens? Woohoo! I couldn't feel prouder.

Little Basil and his brothers and sisters

are four very lucky kittens. They have a loving mum and the Queen of the Kipper Street cats watching over them, not to mention all the other local cats who'll be keeping them safe and teaching them cool cat stuff.

And all they need now is somewhere warm and cosy to rest their little kitten heads.

A NEW HOME

"I can't believe you didn't wake me up!" says Kei, smiling at the squirmy little kittens as they snuggle against their mum under Granny Mo's kitchen table.

"I tried to," I say. Though it's probably a good thing she didn't wake up. Kei would have heard me talking to

cats and badgers and she'd definitely think I was bonkers. Not many people seem to understand animals like I do. "Anyway," I say, "we'll both have plenty of time to play with them now they're living with Granny Mo."

Yes, that's what's happening! Granny Mo found the number for Molly's owners, and earlier this evening they had this big long phone call, and. . . they all think Molly and the kittens should live here. Once the kits are bigger, Molly's owners absolutely want her back. But, in the meantime, I've got new furry neighbours!

Granny Mo and Mum are sipping

cocoa, looking fuzzy-brained. Queen Sardine is out on Kipper Street spreading the exciting news about the kittens. And Molly is drifting in and out of sleep under her nuzzling babies.

"Seems Molly's happy here, doesn't it?" Kei says. "Granny Mo'll have to start thinking about cat food and catnip mice and stuff."

I nod but then suddenly another thought hits me. Right now the kittens are teeny and they don't exactly take up much space. But they won't stay tiny. They'll grow into full-size cats, and then there's no way they can all live here in

Granny Mo's flat. It won't just be Molly leaving, it'll be all of them! Oh, if only Mum and I had room for a cat!

At some point we'll have to say goodbye to our new kitten friends.

"Granny Mo?" I ask. "It's not forever, is it? They can't live here forever, can they?" I soften my voice so (hopefully) Molly can't hear me, and Granny Mo beckons me over for a hug.

"Now, now, Ivy Meadows. Don't be thinking 'bout that tonight. But you're right, I can't be housing five full-grown cats. When the kits are big enough, I'll help Molly's owners find them good homes to go to. Really good homes, okay? You've got nothing to be worryin' about."

Makes sense, I guess. But the thought of saying goodbye seems pretty sad right now.

"It's not for a couple of months," says Mum. "You'll have plenty of time to spend with them before they go to new families. And we'll make sure Molly's ready to let them go first."

"Promise?" I say.

Both Mum and Mo nod and squish me in a cuddle.

"Right, ladies!" says Granny Mo. "It's half past three in the morning. We've got a few hours' sleep to catch before sunrise. Back to the tent or off to bed?"

Oddly, the thought of going back to the tent doesn't bother me any more. "Tent!" I say, without a doubt.

"Maybe," Kei says. "I don't know. . . It was a bit creepy out in the dark, didn't you think?" she asks me. It was creepy for a while, but after my adventures in the garden tonight, it just doesn't feel creepy any more.

"When you woke me up," she says, "and I realised I'd been on my own in the dark...well...yeesh!" Kei shivers and grabs my arm. "Promise you won't leave me in the tent?" she says.

"I promise," I tell her. "Cross my heart. If any more kittens need rescuing I'll yell in your ear and tickle your toes till you wake up. Sound okay?"

She sticks her tongue out at me, with a smile, then we take ourselves back downstairs, back outside, and back to our little garden-home.

When we've wriggled into our sleeping bags and finished off the rest of the Jaffa Cakes, I lie down on my foam roll-mat, switch off both torches and smile to myself in the darkness.

"I'm glad we did this, Kei," I whisper. "Aren't you?...Kei?"

No way – she's done it again! Kei's fallen asleep in record time. No one but no one can fall asleep like Kei can.

I hear Queen Sardine from somewhere outside the tent. "Ivy? Can I come in?"

I shuffle about, unzipping the door, making a comfy nest for her on my

clothes, and she settles down beside me, just as it should be. Me and my best buddy, Queen Sardine, nodding off to sleep, warm and content after a job well done.

TEN WEEKS LATER

It seems like only last night we were bringing Molly and her babies into Granny Mo's flat. But ten weeks on, the kittens are sooo different! They're not squirmy little bundles any more, they've grown up. Now they're proper, mischievous, kitten fluffballs!

Plus they've all got names now. Names I thought of.

First, there's Basil, of course. The littlest of the bunch and still the most likely to disappear and end up in silly places. Like once when he was due to go to the vet's for a check-up, we couldn't find him anywhere for hours. And even though there was no way he could've got out of the flat, we were all starting to get worried, and Molly was prowling up and down mewling for him. So, finally, Granny Mo decided we needed even more light to look for him properly, and she gave her curtains an extra yank to let more sunshine in, when we heard this disgruntled meow! Cos there he was!

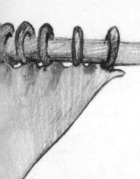

Right on top of the curtain pole. Must've climbed up with his claws and just nodded off to sleep like a cheetah in a tree!

Second, there's Betsy. Betsy's the most like Molly, I think. She's stripy and super-cuddly and likes rolling in the sunshine way more than climbing over Granny Mo's furniture.

Third, there's Barnaby.

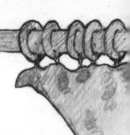

Barnaby's got the loudest purr you ever heard. And he just loves Kei to bits. He follows her around whenever she's here, and he'll perch on her shoulder given half a chance. Kei's mum and dad say she can keep him when it's time for him to leave Molly – which is pretty much now – and

I'm so, so pleased about that. Cos I know he'll be really loved and cared for with Kei.

Last of all there's Belle. Belle is ridiculously pretty, with big blue eyes. To look at her you'd think she was as good as gold, but she's just as mischievous as her brothers and sister. And if you make the mistake of leaving your egg sandwich unguarded on Granny Mo's kitchen table, you can bet Belle will gobble it up in a furry flash!

"Girls," calls Granny Mo from the living room. "Come here a minute."

Kei and I leave the kittens, dropping the feather-on-a-string toy we made for them. We're here most days now, even if it's just for a quick fly-by visit. Queen Sardine too. She checks up on Molly whenever she can. Even brings her little treats from her own dinner bowl sometimes. And she adores the kittens of course. Really loves them!

"Granny?" says Kei.

Granny Mo is sitting on her sofa. Beside her, a cordless phone stands on the coffee table, next to a well-used notebook.

"I've just had a call," she says. "Now, you know I've put the word out about the kittens, trying to find the right homes for them. Well, I've spoken with Molly's owners, and we finally think we've got somewhere for each of them."

Kei and I don't say a word. I can hear their little kitten paws thumping on the hard wood of the floorboards as they jump off the kitchen table. I can hear little kitten meeps and growls as they pretend to fight each other. I don't ever want to stop hearing those wonderful kitten sounds. And when Basil potters in and sits on my foot I think my heart might actually break.

"Kei," says Granny Mo, "you'll be having lil' Barnaby, so that's one of the babes taken care of. But there's the girls to home too, and a kind friend of mine would be very happy to have both of them. She's got a good-sized home, and she lives on a lovely little street. Very safe for cats."

"We live on a lovely street," I say. I don't want to sound all miserable and stubborn, but I can't help it.

"That we do, Ivy. That we do," says Granny Mo with a smile. "And – would you believe it? – our lovely street just so happens to be the same lovely street my friend lives on! And I do believe she's a friend of yours, Ivy Meadows."

She gives me a big wink as

a smile cracks across my face.

"Really?" I cry. "The kittens would still be on Kipper Street?"

Granny Mo nods, chuckling as she speaks. "I think you know Mrs Dodd, don't you?"

Mrs Dodd? I love Mrs Dodd! She's fantastic with cats. She's the old lady who feeds Benny. The one person I know who can talk to cats like I can. Unfortunately her spoilt grandson lives with her too, but she'll make sure Belle and Betsy are well loved, I know she will.

"Brilliant!" I say, just as Basil springs

from my left foot and tumbles onto my right. Basil. . . my heart sinks again. Barnaby's going to live with Kei. Belle and Betsy are moving in with Mrs Dodd. What are the chances of Basil also going to someone I could actually visit? Probably about one in a billion-gazillion.

My eyes prickle with tears and suddenly all those fears I had about camping in the dark feel so silly. Now I'm scared. Scared of losing Basil. And that fear's so much worse than headless owls and imaginary monsters of the night.

"I suspect you'll be wondering 'bout this lil' fella, huh?" Granny Mo says, and I nod. I can feel the edges of my mouth slumping down, and try as I might, I can't force a smile.

"The thing is," she says, "there's no way I could house five grown cats in this flat."

Kei squeezes my hand and says softly, "We know, Granny."

"But one cat. . . Yes, I think perhaps I could manage one."

It takes a moment for what she's saying to sink in. Granny Mo could manage one cat… "Basil?! You're keeping Basil?"

Kei squeals with delight and Basil jumps onto Granny Mo's knee for safety. "Yes, I thought I might," laughs Mo. "Molly's owners offered him to me as a 'thank-you' for looking after the lot o' dem. An' how could I say no? I've grown soft on the cheeky lil' thing."

I can't even speak. I could squeal with delight but I don't want to spook Basil, so I make little kissy noises instead, and soon he comes

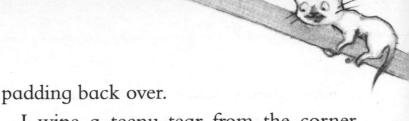

padding back over.

I wipe a teeny tear from the corner of my eye and hope no one notices how soppy I'm being. I just can't help it. He's staying! Basil – the cheekiest kitten in Kipper Street – is staying. Staying for good.

I have to tell Queen Sardine!

Lifting Basil into Kei's arms I tell him, "I'll be right back." I dash downstairs to find Her Majesty.

And of course she's not far away. She's never far from Molly and the kittens these days. So it's really no surprise that she's already here, waiting. I open Granny

Mo's door at the bottom of the stairs and she potters in.

She brushes past me as I blurt, "Oh, Your Majesty! I've got the best news ever!" But she's distracted by something. "Quick, shut the door, Ivy," Sardine says, looking up the stairs behind me. "Little Lord Cheeky Pants is trying to escape."

Meow! Meeeeeeow!

It's Basil. He's jumping down the stairs, one by one, coming to join us. I pull the door until it clicks, but I don't think she's right. I don't think Basil wants to go outside. I think

he wants to see his favourite queen.

"Oh, really!" she moans as Basil biffs at her paws, but she's smiling all the while. Queen Sardine likes playing with him. She just likes acting all prim and regal too.

Basil then decides to climb on her, and Her Majesty gives in. She lies on the ground, flat on her tummy, and lets the little terror clamber onto her back. "You were saying?" she sighs. "Something about news?"

"Yes!" I say. "It's brilliant! It's Basil. He's—"

"Meow!" Basil interrupts. "Meeeeeow!" he says, right into Queen Sardine's ear.

"Oh, Basil, that's quite enough!" she says. Then, "Sorry, Ivy. Please do go on."

"Meow!" Basil insists. "Meeeeeeow!" he squeals, like he wants to tell her something.

And then the most amazing thing

happens. He does tell her something. . .

"Meow! Meeeeeow! Meeee-stay!" he says. He really says it. *Me stay.*

"Was that. . .? Did he just. . .?" Her Majesty gasps.

My jaw's gone all slack with surprise, and all I can do is nod. But I know exactly what Sardine's trying to ask. Did Basil just say his first words? And yep, yes, yessiree, he absolutely did.

Meeeee stay!

"You're staying, Basil? Staying for good?"

Queen Sardine asks him, twisting her head to look up at the determined little moggy.

"Meeeee stay!" he says again. "Me stay."

"Well, that's just… that's just. . ." Oh dear. Her Majesty seems to be sobbing. Good grief, I thought she'd be pleased!

I sit on the stair beside her, and heave her onto my lap, with Basil still attached.

"Are you okay?" I ask softly. I stroke her fur while she sniffs and swallows. Poor Basil must be so confused by all this. I know I am.

Then in choked-up, broken words, she says, "That's just perfectly, perfectly. . . purrrfect!" And I get it now. Of course I do. They were sobs of joy. Happy sniffles. "Oh, Ivy, this is the best news — ever! Why didn't you say?"

I seem to remember trying to say. But is it any wonder she didn't notice? I mean, with the world's cutest kitten doing super-clever stuff like saying his first words — to us! — how could she notice anything else?

And so with sobs and snuggles, tickles and hugs, we sit here. Huddled up on the stair. All three of us.

Some of us purring.
One of us grinning.
All of us simply, totally. . .
Happy.